Speed Bikes

T

David Orme

Published in 2002 by:
Nelson Thornes Ltd
Delta Place
27 Bath Road
CHELTENHAM
GL53 7TH
United Kingdom

02 03 04 05 06 / 10 9 8 7 6 5 4 3 2 1

A catalogue record for this book is available from the British Library

ISBN 0-7487-6406-2

Illustrations by Beverly Curl
Cover illustration by Richard Garland (represented by Advocate)
Page make-up by Peter Nickol

Printed and bound in Great Britain by T. J. International

Contents

Chapter 1

At the limit

The 500cc engines roared like trapped tigers. The start tape flew up, and the four bikes were off!

Lee Clark was in a good second place. He was brilliant on the slides. To do well in speedway this was a vital skill.

Speedway was an important part of Lee's life. He felt that the bike was a part of him as he flew round the oval track.

With no brakes or gears, bikers had to rely on a strong left foot and their skill. You had to ride at the limit all the time – and over the limit.

Sometimes you got away with it, and sometimes you didn't. Lee had had minor injuries — but so far, nothing serious had happened to him.

Lee had been in all sorts of trouble before he took up biking. He had been suspended from school, then excluded for good. He got involved with a group of troublemakers and was in trouble with the police. He had been lucky not to get youth custody.

Then a friend had taken him to watch Southway Stars speedway. He liked it, and got involved. He had discovered something he was really good at. Since then he had stayed out of trouble.

"I used to get angry about things," Lee thought. "I wanted to take it out on people by smashing things up. Now if I feel angry, I ride speedway. Then I don't feel angry any more."

The leading rider had started brilliantly. It was going to be tough to catch him up.

Lee hit the throttle. He was sideways now, controlling the slide with his free left foot.

Then he lost it. A bit too much gas, control that wasn't quite perfect. He went sliding into the barrier. The bike stalled. He was out of the race.

Lee picked himself up. A few more bruises, but no bones broken! He didn't mind about the crash. It was only a midweek practice session. He knew that he could learn from his mistakes.

Chapter 2

Bad news

Southway Stars were getting ready for an important race at the weekend. They were riding against Blackstone Panthers in the local league. Panthers were the Stars' greatest rivals. They came from the next town along the coast.

Panthers had a sponsor who put a lot of money into the team. The latest bikes, fancy clothes and helmets, the lot. They had won the local championship last year. The Stars team desperately wanted to beat them.

At the end of the session they met up in the team garage. They expected the team boss, Reg

French, to talk them through the practice. But he had other things to say.

"Listen up, lads. I've got some bad news. I've had a letter from the new owner of the stadium. He's given us notice to get out of here at the end of the season. They're going to pull down the stadium and build houses here instead!"

The team couldn't believe the news.

"I thought the council owned the stadium," said Ricky.

"They did," said Reg. "But they've sold it to a firm called John Herbert plc. He's got the old factory site next door, too. The whole area is going to be a housing estate. There's nowhere else for us to go. At the end of the season, the club's finished. Sorry guys, there's nothing I can do."

Chapter 3

A terrible anger

Walking home, Lee felt a terrible anger inside him. It was a good thing he was with Ricky and Daniel. He felt he wanted to smash something, but the company of his friends stopped him going back to his old ways.

"Don't let it get to you, Lee," pleaded Ricky. "Something'll turn up."

Lee knew Ricky was just trying to be cheerful. They all knew there wasn't much hope.

The race meeting started as planned on Saturday. The team was determined to do well.

"If we've got to go, let's go out with a bang," said Reg.

Blackstone Panthers were a pretty decent team, but the Stars didn't think so!

"It's all right for them," said Daniel. "They've got a big sponsor and somewhere to ride."

Panthers won the meeting – but only just! Their manager said it was the toughest challenge they had had all year.

"I'm sorry to hear your news," he said to Reg. "It's a tough world. We've got to find a new sponsor next year. Won't be easy."

After the race, the team found Reg talking to a man they didn't know.

"Right, gang," he said. "I want you to meet someone. This is John Herbert."

Chapter 4

A quiet word

The property developer made it very clear that he wasn't going to change his mind.

"This stadium would need a lot of money spent on it to bring it up to standard. Anyway, I've got to sell houses on the factory site. No one wants to live next to a noisy speedway track."

Lee lost his temper. He couldn't hold back. He said something rude – very rude.

Mr Herbert went white with anger.

"I came here to see if I could help out. But if that's how you feel, I'll say goodnight."

Lee realised he had been stupid — he had blown it for all of them. But Reg came to the rescue.

"Just a quiet word, please, Mr Herbert."

He took Mr Herbert into his office. Outside, the rest of the team told Lee what they thought of him. They were ruder still.

The office door opened.

"Come on in here, young Clark," said Reg. "I want to give you the chance to apologise."

Lee got up reluctantly and went into the office, closing the door behind him.

"Sorry, Mr Herbert," he said.

"OK lad, let's forget it. Reg has told me a bit about you. Now I'm going to tell you about me. I was like you once. Always in trouble. I even did a spell in prison. But bikes were always my thing, like they are to you. I didn't have the chance to do anything about it, though.

"You can see I've done well. I want to put something back. I can't let you keep the

stadium, but I've got a plan. We might be able to solve the problem, if you'll accept my help. Let's see what the others think."

They went back out into the garage. Mr Herbert spoke to the whole group.

"This is my offer. Blackstone Panthers have just lost their sponsor. They asked me to help them. But I want to help you too. How would you feel about being part of the best team in the south of England?"

Chapter 5

As good as his word

They liked the sound of that, until they realised what it would mean. They would have to join up with the Panthers!

"So they can just take our best riders, and dump the rest of us?" said Ricky angrily.

Mr Herbert was not a patient man, but he did his best.

"Stop thinking small, lads! You're good riders – too good for this local league of yours. I want to build a side for the national league – the best team in the country, maybe even a world beater. This is a great chance for all of

you – but you'll have to swallow your pride."

"And the two teams go in as equals?" asked Daniel.

"Absolutely."

Mr Herbert was as good as his word. The following season the Southern All Stars were launched – and they were a success right away. A year later Lee became team captain. Some of the speedway meetings were on television, and he became quite a star – it certainly helped when it came to getting girlfriends!

One evening Mr Herbert had come to watch the team. He called Lee over after the racing.

"I've been meaning to ask – apart from speedway, what do you do?"

"It's hard to hold down a real job. Speedway takes up a lot of time."

"Thought so. You need a career, you know. Speedway doesn't last for ever!"

Lee shrugged.

"How about coming to work for me?"

Lee wasn't sure.

"Go for it, lad! I was just like you. Now I'm a millionaire. I told you before – don't think small!"

He didn't. Many years later, an old man and a middle-aged man watched speedway together. The Southern All Stars were still winning, and on their gear was the name of their sponsor – Herbert & Clark plc.

If you like this book, you may also enjoy others from the same series.

Up For It! (Football)
Trail Bikes (Mountain biking)
Snow Trek (Snowboarding)
Hot Skates (Ice hockey)
Head to Head (Sprint relay)
A Crazy Sport (Triathlon)

Rock Face (Rock climbing)
Speed Bikes (Speedway)
Running into Trouble (Marathon)
Skating to Danger (Outdoor skating)
Hit It! (Water skiing)
Goalie's Nightmare (Football)

Match Ref (Football   coaching, refereeing)
Dive and Survive (Sea diving)
Pit Stop (Formula 1)
Deep Trouble (Potholing)
In at the Deep End (Swimming)
Close to the Wind (Windsurfing)